Damien and the Dragon Kite

Author:Raymond Macalino
Illustrator:András Balogh

CRYSTAL
MOSAIC
BOOKS

This is a work of fiction. All of the characters and events portrayed in this story are products of the author's imagination. Any resemblance to actual events or persons, living or dead, is entirely coincidental.

DAMIEN AND THE DRAGON KITE

Text and illustration:
Copyright © 2012 Raymond Macalino

Illustrated by András Balogh

For information, address Crystal Mosaic Books,
PO Box 1276 Hillsboro, OR 97123.

ISBN: 978-0-9836303-6-4

Get Your Free Book!

Join the Super Secret Reader List and get a free copy of

The Wish Fish Activity Book

part of The Wish Fish Early Reader Series.

Super Secret Readers get free books, posters, videos, and all kinds of other great goodies, so hop on over to

www.macalino.com

and sign up today!

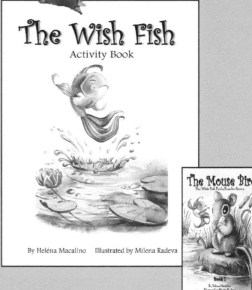

The Wish Fish
Activity Book

By Heléna Macalino   Illustrated by Milena Radeva

The Mouse Bird
The Wish Fish Early Reader Series

The adventure has just begun!

To my precious two...
An endless source of inspiration.

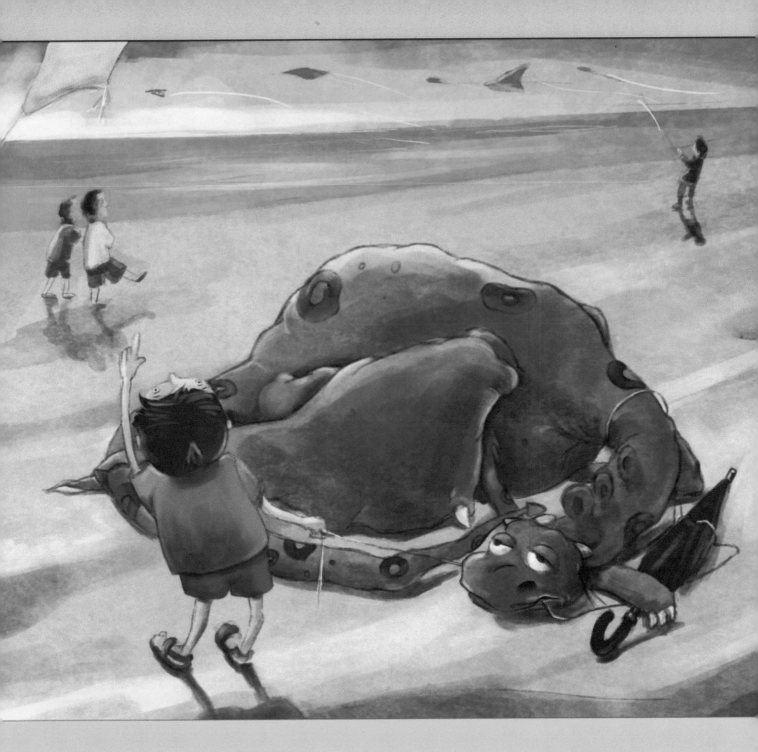

Get Your Free Book!

Join the Super Secret Reader List and get a free copy of

The Wish Fish Activity Book

part of The Wish Fish Early Reader Series.

Super Secret Readers get free books, posters, videos, and all kinds of other great goodies, so hop on over to
www.macalino.com
and sign up today!

Don't let the adventure end!

Draw a dragon

Draw two eggs. These will be the head and body of the dragon.

Draw the neck, legs, and tail.

Draw the eyes.

Draw the nose and mouth.

Draw the scales on the head and neck.

Draw the scales on the tail.

Draw the hair.

Draw the wings.

Finally, draw the spots!

Labyrinth

Help Damien's dragon find his way
through the clouds!

Finish

Magic Dot-to-Dot

Join the dots to complete Damien's dragon then color it with your favorite color!

ABOUT THE AUTHOR:

Raymond Macalino works full time as a Program Manager for a software company in Portland, Oregon. When not working in the corporate world, he spends time with his wife and kids conjuring up stories and letting imagination take us where it may.

You can reach Raymond at raymond.macalino@gmail.com.

ABOUT THE ILLUSTRATOR:

András Balogh is a children's book illustrator and digital painter. He has more than 10 years experience in traditional painting and is a full member of the Society of Children's Book Writers and Illustrators.

András studied at the Free School of Fine Arts Kecskemét in Hungary where he received a strong foundation in the arts, visual creativity, traditional painting, anatomy, and descriptive geometry.

You can reach András at illusztratio@gmail.com.

Look for Raymond Macalino's next children's illustrated book, about a pig on a lonely planet, whose life is changed forever when he is visited by some unexpected visitors.

CPSIA information can be obtained
at www.ICGtesting.com
Printed in the USA
LVHW071122171219
640775LV00011B/432/P